It's Your First Day of School, Busy Bus!

It's Your First Day

written by

Jody Jensen Shaffer

# of School, Busy Bus!

illustrated by

Claire Messer

BEACH LANE BOOKS · New York   London   Toronto   Sydney   New Delhi

Ben the bus driver opens the doors of the bus barn.
"Good morning, everyone!" he says.
"Busy Bus, it's your first day of school!"

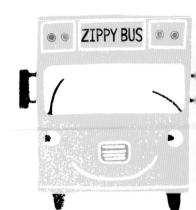

Busy Bus is wide awake.
He can't wait to meet the children!
He hopes they will like him.

BOUNCY BUS

BIG BUS

HONK!

"Let's make **sure** you're ready to go," says Ben.

He measures the air in Busy Bus's tires.

Pssssss!

GAS

He fills Busy Bus's tank with gas.

Gussshhhh!

Then he swivels Busy Bus's mirrors.
"Now we can see everything," he says.

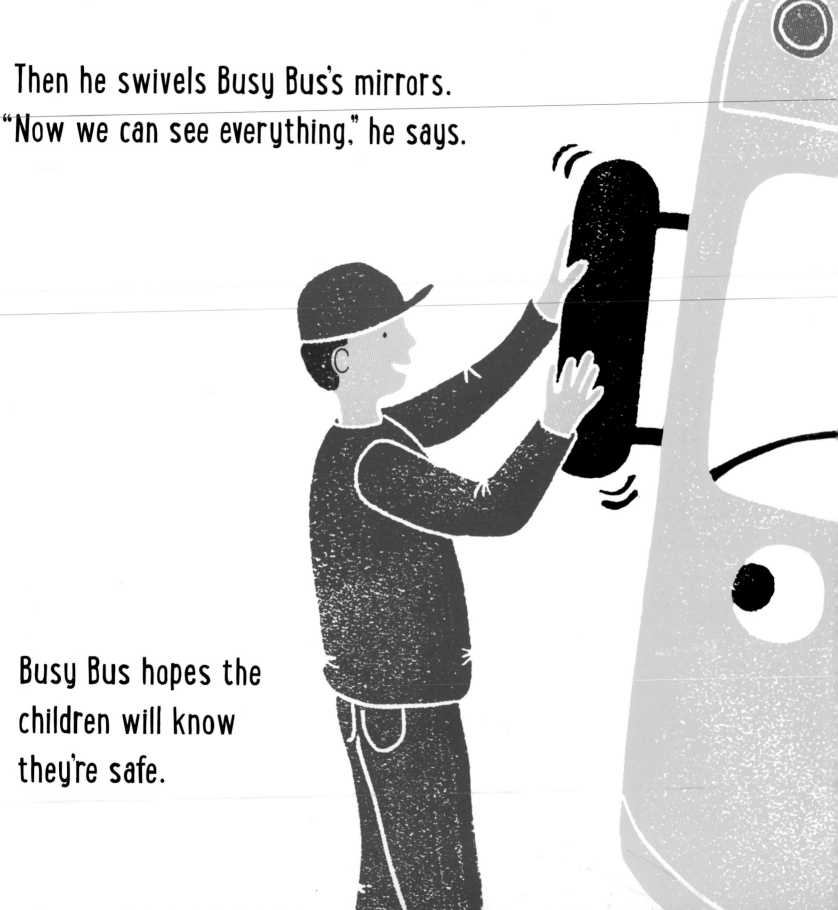

Busy Bus hopes the children will know they're safe.

"Okay, Busy Bus. Let's keep checking," says Ben.

He moves Busy Bus's stop arm.

He inspects the emergency door,

the fire extinguisher,

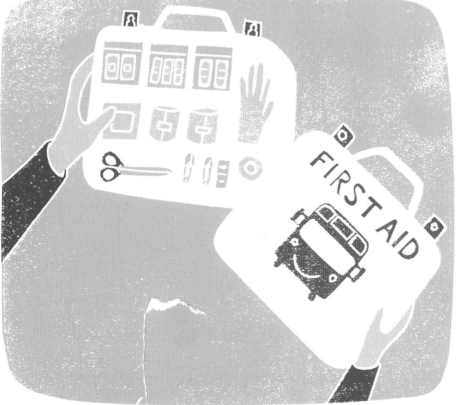

and the first aid kit.

Will the children have fun riding with me?
Busy Bus wonders.

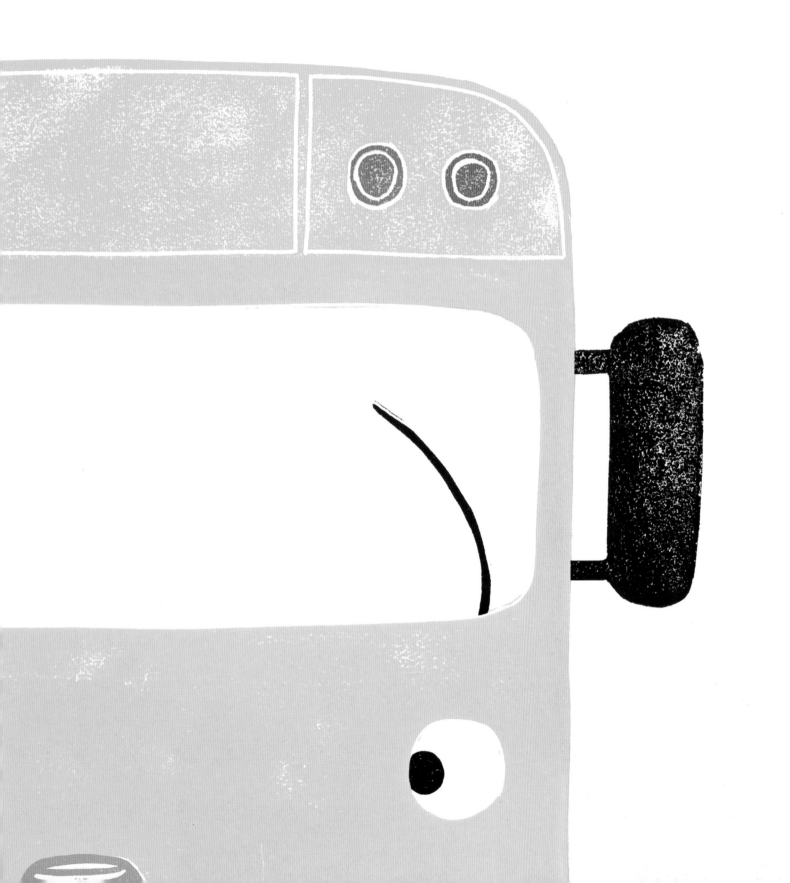

"We're almost finished, Busy Bus. Let's check your engine."
Ben turns the key. Busy Bus *purrrrs* like a kitten!

Ben looks at the buttons and gauges on the dashboard.
He tries Busy Bus's wipers, steering wheel, and brakes.

rrr!

HONK!

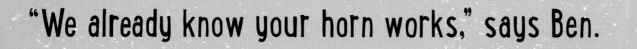

"We already know your horn works," says Ben.

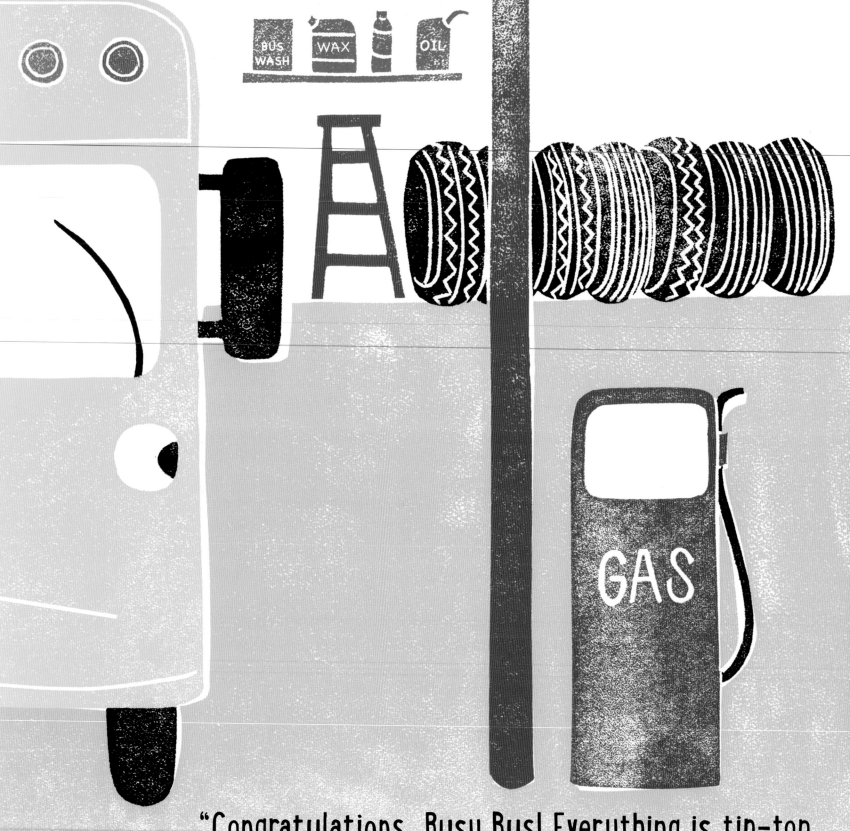

"Congratulations, Busy Bus! Everything is tip-top.
Let's go get the children."

But Busy Bus isn't so sure.

What if I get homesick? he worries.

What if I don't make any friends?

"I almost forgot!" says Ben.

"This is for you, Busy Bus."

Now Busy Bus is ready for his first day of school.

He is safe.

He is clean.

He is loved.

Busy Bus is going to
have a great year!

For Madeline and Sam and all your firsts
—J. J. S.

For Kirsten
—C. M.

BEACH LANE BOOKS An imprint of Simon & Schuster Childrens Publishing Division · 1230 Avenue of the Americas. New York. New York 10020
Text copyright © 2018 by Jody Jensen Shaffer · Illustrations copyright © 2018 by Claire Messer
For information about special discounts for bulk purchases. please contact Simon & Schuster Special Sales
at 1-866-506-1949 or business@simonandschuster.com. · The Simon & Schuster Speakers Bureau can bring authors to your live event.
For more information or to book an event. contact the Simon & Schuster Speakers Bureau at 1-866-248-3049 or visit our website at www.simonspeakers.com.
Book design by Lauren Rille · The text for this book was set in LunchBox Regular. · The illustrations for this book were created with lino prints and black ink and then
colored digitally. · Manufactured in China · 0418 SCP · First Edition · 10 9 8 7 6 5 4 3 2 1
Library of Congress Cataloging-in-Publication Data
Names: Shaffer. Jody Jensen. author. | Messer. Claire. illustrator.
Title: It's your first day of school. Busy Bus! / Jody Jensen Shaffer ; illustrated by Claire Messer. · Other titles: It is your first day of school. Busy Bus! · Description:
First edition. | New York : Beach Lane Books. [2018] | Summary: "Today is the very first day of school! Busy Bus is excited. but he also has some first-day jitters.
Luckily. bus driver Ben knows just what to do to make sure that the school year gets off to a great start"—Provided by publisher. · Identifiers: LCCN 2017037359 |
ISBN 9781481494670 (hardcover : alk. paper) | · ISBN 9781481494687 (eBook) · Subjects: | CYAC: First day of school—Fiction. | School buses—Fiction.
Classification: LCC PZ7.1.S4745 It 2018 | DDC [E]—dc23 LC record available at https://lccn.loc.gov/2017037359

HONK!